W9-BZY-236

Larry Burkett's
Great Smoky Mountains Storybook Series

A Different Kind of Party

Written by
Larry Burkett
with **K. Christie Bowler**

Illustrated by **Terry Julien**

MOODY PRESS
CHICAGO

Dedicated to
Israel (Izzy) and Eon Burkett

Text & Illustrations ©1999 BURKETT & KIDS, LLC

Larry Burkett's Money Matters for Kids™
Executive Producer: *Allen Burkett*

For Lightwave
Managing Editor: *Elaine Osborne*
Art Director: *Terry Van Roon*
Desktop: *Andrew Jaster*

All rights reserved. No part of this book may be reproduced in any form without permission in writing from the publisher, except in the case of brief quotations embodied in critical articles or reviews.

Scripture taken from the *Holy Bible: New International Reader's Version®*. NIrV®. Copyright ©1994, 1996 by International Bible Society. Used by permission of Zondervan Publishing House. All rights reserved.

The "NIrV" and "New International Reader's Version" trademarks are registered in the United States Patent and Trademark Office by International Bible Society. Use of either trademark requires permission of International Bible Society.

ISBN: 0-8024-0983-0
1 3 5 9 10 8 6 4 2
Printed in the United States of America

The Great Smoky Mountain Tales come to you from Larry Burkett's Money Matters for Kids™. In each tale, our family's children have fun while they learn how to best manage their money according to God's principles of stewardship.

This series of children's stories tells the adventures of the Carmichael family who live in a state park in the Great Smoky Mountains of North Carolina. The park is a beautiful setting, with a mist rising from the mountains like a smoky mist, giving them their name. Mom and Dad work in the park and, with their children Sarah, Joshua, and Carey, live in the rangers' compound not far inside the main park gate. Sarah, ten years old, is conscientious and loves doing things the right way. She has lots of energy, is artistic, and thinks before she acts. Her brother Joshua is eight and a half. Always doing something active, he's impulsive, adventurous, and eager to learn. Carey, their younger sister, is almost three and very cute. She loves doing whatever her sister and brother are doing. In the first four books of the series they learn how to save, how to give to the church, how to spend wisely, and how to earn money.

There's always something interesting going on in the Great Smoky Mountains, from hiking and horseback riding to fishing or panning for sapphires and rubies. Nearby, the town of Waynesville and, only a little farther away, the city of Asheville, provide all the family needs in the way of city amenities.

Through everyday adventures—from buying pet hamsters to dealing with the aftermath of a winter storm, from getting the right equipment in order to become an artist to going on summer camping trips—the children learn. Practical situations any child could face serve as the background for teaching about God's principles of stewardship.

Your children will love the stories and ask for more. Without even realizing it, they will, like our characters, learn in the middle of an adventure.

Thunder rumbled and shook the house. Lightning lit up the family room for a second, catching three young faces staring out of the window. A cozy fire crackling in the fireplace sent wavering shadows across the room. Joshua sighed dreamily. "I love storms," he said. "They're so cool!"

"Yeah," Sarah agreed, "they're cool from inside the house."

Sarah's friend Maria nodded. "I'm glad we're not out there." They all had the next day, Friday, off from school, so Maria was spending the night. She lived in Waynesville and loved coming out to the state park where Sarah's family lived.

Mom carried in a tray of hot chocolate and cookies and set it down on the coffee table. "It's a great night to be cozy by the fire," she said with a smile.

"Cozy fire," Carey agreed. She plopped herself down on the carpet in front of the blaze.

Leaving the window, Joshua asked, "When will Dad be home?"

"Soon. He's helping to clear branches off the road. There's a strong wind tonight."

The children gathered around the fireplace in their pajamas to drink their hot chocolate.

Just as the kids finished their hot chocolate and cookies and were about to go to bed, the door banged open and closed. Dad came in, dripping wet. He removed his coat and shoes and then stood by the fire, rubbing his hands together.

"It's quite a storm out there," he said as Mom handed him some hot chocolate. He sipped, then closed his eyes and sighed, "Ah. That's good." He smiled at the kids. "Some branches blew onto the road, but they missed the wires, thank goodness. We got the main ones cleared away. The rest we'll do tomorrow."

"Can I help you, Dad?" Joshua asked.

"We'll see," Dad said. "Tom's car wouldn't start, so I drove him home, then swung by the church. Looks like the wind blew some shingles off the roof and a falling branch did a little damage."

"Is there a hole right through?" Sarah asked, her eyes big.

"No. But if the rain keeps up, it might leak. It will have to be fixed."

"Will the pastor fix it?" Joshua asked. "What will he use?"

"He'll buy shingles with some of the money we take to church on Sundays," Dad answered.

"You can fix a roof with the money we put in the offering?" Sarah asked doubtfully.

"And more!" Mom answered. "The money we put in is used to take care of the church and everything it's involved in."

Dad explained, "Everyone who is part of the church puts in money. It's our community. That means it's our responsibility. We all have to do our part to take care of the church. Together, our work and money help the church do what God told it to."

"You give money to your church?" Maria asked in surprise. "Why?"

"God told us to, right?" Sarah said.

Mom nodded. "We give our money to the church out of obedience. It's like our family. We help pay its bills."

The next morning, Dad took Sarah, Maria, and Joshua to the church to look at the damage. They could see where the shingles had been torn off. Joshua found a couple in the parking lot.

"Do you want to see where the money you bring goes?" Dad asked. When the children nodded, he led them inside. Dad knocked on the pastor's door. "I'm showing the kids what their money does," he said.

Pastor Randall smiled and offered to take over the tour. "Lights," he said, pointing. Then he pointed out other things that had to be paid for: the photocopier, telephone, receptionist, bulletin, hymn books, and music equipment.

"Wow!" Maria said. "You guys pay for all this?"

Dad laughed. "Along with everyone else who gives their money to the church. And we pay the pastor's salary so he can pay his bills, and buy groceries and clothes and gas for his car."

Joshua pointed, "Hey look!" A bucket was sitting on the floor catching drips of water. The pastor nodded. "We'll have to fix the roof soon."

After they left the church, Dad surprised them by stopping at the ice-cream parlor. Over a cone, Sarah said, "Just think, if we didn't bring our money to church, the pastor might run out of gas!"

"You're right," Joshua said. "What if we forgot?"

"Don't worry," Dad comforted them. "God will take care of the pastor and his family."

Maria frowned. "How come you take your money there when you don't live there or get anything for it? I mean, it's not like a store where you give them money and you get candy or something."

"But we do get things for our money," Dad said. "We learn more about God. We get a nice place to worship God in and meet with our friends."

"We get Vacation Bible School and Kids' Club and stuff," Sarah added.

Maria shrugged, "I've got lots of things I want to get with my money. I think I'll keep it."

Dad smiled. "That's up to you, Maria. Why don't you come to church with us on Sunday and check it out?"

Deep in thought, Joshua finished his ice cream and asked, "But we don't give to the church just to get stuff, do we?"

Dad smiled and led them back out to the car. "No. When we give to the church, we're giving back to God. It's a way of saying 'thank-you' for all the good things He gives us and how well He takes care of us."

Maria looked surprised. "God gives you stuff? Like what?"

"Everything," Dad answered. "God made it all and lets us use it. He makes sure we have everything we really need. He helped me get my job. He makes food grow so we'll have something to eat. When we give some of what God gives us back to Him by giving it to His church, we're showing that we trust Him to look after us."

"Wow!" Maria said. "I didn't know God was looking after you guys."

"Cool, huh!" Sarah commented.

"God likes doing it," Dad added. "He wants to look after everyone. You, too."

On the way home, Dad stopped at the Food Bank. "This is another thing the church does with our money," he said, leading the children inside. Food lined the walls and people were being served free meals. "Want to help?"

"Sure."

"You can wash the dishes and clear the tables." The kids groaned but got to work. Sarah put too much soap in the sink and it foamed up . . . and up. Soon they were having a soap-bubble fight. Later, they had juice and cookies.

"The church uses some of our money to buy food and serve the people who can't buy their own," Dad explained. "Your money blesses people all around Waynesville. Not only that," he added with a grin, "it blesses people around the world. We send some to Africa to help the missionaries tell people about God, treat the sick, and teach them to read the Bible."

"Wow!" Joshua said. "I thought it just stayed at church 'til God picked it up." The others laughed.

That Sunday Maria joined the family at church. A pot beside the bench next to Joshua was catching drips. Joshua nudged his sister. "They better fix the roof soon," he said, pointing to the ceiling.

Just then the offering plate was passed down their row. Joshua and Sarah put their money in, thinking about all the things it would be used for.

Pastor Randall gave the announcements. Then he said, "You might have noticed that we had some damage from the last storm. We have enough money in the maintenance fund to buy the materials to fix the leak. But we don't have quite enough to pay a professional roofer to do the job."

Dad raised his hand. When the pastor asked him to speak, Dad stood up. "Pastor, we have people in our congregation who know how to fix a roof. Why don't we have a 'roof-fixing' party and all pitch in? After all, it's our community. We give God our time and abilities as well as our money."

Others nodded and said, "Yeah. Good idea. Let's do it." So the "roof-fixing" party was arranged for the next Saturday.

Saturday dawned clear and sunny. The whole family, including Carey, helped Mom make sandwiches and pack a big picnic lunch. On the way to the church for the roof-fixing party, they picked up Maria—and some balloons.

They arrived to find the place hopping. Two pickup trucks full of shingles, nails, and ladders were being unloaded. Dad joined the others who were going to help with the roof, and the kids ran off to find their friends and see what was happening.

Mom took their food into the basement. While people visited, they organized the food, heated it up, fixed tea and coffee, and prepared snacks. The kids were given chores they could do, like rake the lawn, wash windows, or help put snacks on trays and take cups upstairs. When everything was ready to go, they all stopped for a snack and a drink.

Maria was surprised at how much fun she was having. Suddenly Joshua and another kid threw a water balloon at her. She screamed and jumped. The water fight spread quickly until it included most of the adults.

After the snack, things really started moving! The crew who knew how to fix a roof climbed up the ladders to the piles of shingles set out for them. They had to remove the old loose or cracked shingles and then fix the new ones in place.

The roof-fixing party turned into a general fix-it party. Those who weren't on the roof got to work on whatever other jobs were needed. Some worked on the back stairs, some strengthened rickety pews, and some even painted a couple of the Sunday school rooms.

Outside, the kids were working in the yard, pulling weeds, raking and jumping in the last of the fall leaves,

cutting the grass, and whatever needed doing to get the church ready for winter. Everyone was having a great time.

Maria turned to Sarah. "Now I know what your Dad meant. Giving isn't just about money. It's about belonging to a community too," she said. "This is great! I never knew you could have this much fun working."

Sarah laughed. "Yeah. Come on. We can jump in the leaves again before we bag them."

As the afternoon wore on, clouds gathered and it started to look like rain. The roofers sped up. They needed to be finished before the rain came. Finally, they were done! They straightened up and examined their work. Satisfied, they grinned at each other and gathered up the extra nails and left-over shingles. Just as Dad climbed down the ladder, the first raindrops fell.

"Just in time," Joshua said, running up.

Dad stretched. "Yup. It seems like God timed it just right."

As the men and women cleaned up and put their tools away, the rain really started coming down. They finished quickly and ran for the church.

The basement smelled delicious! A full pot-luck meal was waiting for them. Pastor Randall thanked everyone for their help and then prayed, "Thank you, Father, for holding the rain off and for good friends. Thank you for providing the food and all the gifts and blessings You've given us. In Jesus' name, amen."

As soon as he said, "Amen," people dug into the food.

The next day there were no pots by the pews to catch the leaks.

Maria joined the family in church again. She had decided she liked this place. And the people were great! She'd had more fun the day before than she'd expected. She nudged Sarah. "Can I be part of your church?" she asked.

Sarah nodded. "Of course! It's really God's church, you know. He'd love you to come."

"I'd like to learn about God," Maria said. "And I can give some of my money to help keep things going, right?"

Sarah smiled. "Yeah. But even if you couldn't, you could still come."

"Well," Maria whispered, "I figure your Dad was right. I figure God gave me all kinds of good things. I'd like to thank Him too."

When the offering plate came by, Maria put the money she'd brought into it, thinking of all the good things it would be used for. Then she prayed quietly, "Thank you, God, for taking care of me like you do Sarah's family. And please help me become Your child like Sarah and Joshua are. In Jesus' name, amen."

That afternoon Dad made a big bowl of popcorn. Mom brought juice in and the family and Maria gathered around.

"Yesterday was fun," Maria told them. "I didn't know you could have so much fun at church. Or working!"

Dad laughed. "When we all pitch in and do our part in the church, it works well. And everyone enjoys themselves."

"And learns," Mom added. "Our money pays for the building and everything needed to keep the church going, but it also pays for the teaching we get. It helps us learn how to get closer to God and live life the way He designed it. That's one of the Pastor's main jobs."

"Sometimes our money provides furniture, food, or clothes for people without them," Dad added.

"Our money's pretty busy, huh?" Joshua asked. "Does it make God happy?"

"Absolutely. He knows we give back to Him because we're grateful and trust Him. He loves it that we're helping the church do what He wants it to."

Tithe to Give!

"You should each give what you have decided in your heart to give. You shouldn't give if you don't want to. You shouldn't give because you are forced to. God loves a cheerful giver" (2 Corinthians 9:7 NirV). (Check out Luke 11:42.)

Church is God's idea. He's given it to you for your good, to teach you, encourage you, guide you, and help you. You learn about Him there. And God's given each person ways to be a part of the church and help out. One way you can help is by giving some of your money or your time and talents.

The Envelope Please!

Tithing to your church is simple. But if you don't have a plan for what you do with your money, now's a good time to start. Here's a simple one: Put ten percent (tithe means a tenth or ten percent) of your money, or ten cents of every dollar you get, into a Tithing envelope or bank. Forty percent, or forty cents out of every dollar, goes into your Spending envelope or bank for you to spend any way you want. Put the other fifty percent (fifty cents out of every dollar) in your Savings envelope or bank for things you want to buy but can't afford right now. Then follow these simple steps to giving to the church.

1. Whenever you get money, divide it up into your different envelopes.
2. Decide if you're going to take your money to church every week or once a month. Then, the night before church or early in the morning, empty your Tithing envelope or bank into one of the special envelopes your church provides. Write your name and the amount on it.
3. Take your envelope to church and put it into the offering plate.

4. Celebrate. While you're getting ready to give your money and while you're putting it in the offering, thank God for how good He is to you and how well He takes care of you.
5. Take a church envelope home with you for next week or month.

But you don't have to stop with 10 percent. Sometimes your church takes up special offerings for people in need or special missions' projects. That's a great opportunity to give extra to help what God's doing in the world. So take some money out of your Spending envelope or bank and take that to the church as a gift.

Own It

Remember, the church is not just a building or a mission. It's people. It's your community. It's the place your friends are, the place you're taught about Jesus, God, and the Christian life. You're part of it and it's part of you.

When you say, "Our house" or "Our home," you're talking about ownership. It belongs to you and your family, and you're responsible for it. It's up to you to take care of it, make sure it's in good shape, pay the bills, and so on. What would happen if you never looked after it? Soon it would be in pretty bad shape and you'd be without electricity or a phone! It's the same with church. When you say "Our church," you're saying it belongs to you and you're responsible for it. So enjoy looking after the place that is such a big part of your life.

Larry Burkett's Money Matters for Kids™ provides practical tips and tools children need to understand the biblical principles of stewardship. **Money Matters for Kids™** is committed to the next generation and is grounded in God's Word and living His principles. Its goal is *"Teaching Kids to Manage God's Gifts."*

Money Matters for Kids™ and **Money Matters for Teens™** materials are adapted by **Lightwave Publishing™** from the works of best selling author on business and personal finances, **Larry Burkett.** Larry is the founder and president of **Christian Financial Concepts™**, author of more than 50 books, and hosts a radio program "Money Matters" aired on more than 1,100 outlets worldwide. Money Matters for Kids™ has an entertaining and educational Web site for children, teens, and college students, along with a special **Financial Parenting™** Resource section for adults.

Visit Money Matters for Kids Web site at: **www.mm4kids.org**

building Christian faith in families

Lightwave Publishing is a recognized leader in developing quality resources that encourage, assist, and equip parents to build Christian faith in their families.

Lightwave Publishing also has a fun kids' Web site and an internet-based newsletter called *Tips & Tools for Spiritual Parenting.* This newsletter helps parents with issues such as answering their children's questions, helping make church more exciting, teaching children how to pray, and much more.

For more information, visit Lightwave's Web site: **www.lightwavepublishing.com**

MOODY
The Name You Can Trust
A MINISTRY OF MOODY BIBLE INSTITUTE

Moody Press, a ministry of Moody Bible Institute, is designed for education, evangelization, and edification.

If we may assist you in knowing more about Christ and the Christian life, please write us without obligation:

Moody Press, c/o MLM Chicago, Illinois 60610.

Or visit us at Moody's Web site: **www.moodypress.org**